The Secret Ballroom

by

Susi Moore

The Secret Ballroom © 2015 Susi Moore.

The Secret Ballroom © 2015 Susi Moore. All Rights Reserved.
ISBN 978-1544167763

No part of this work or publication may be reproduced in any form without the prior written permission of the copyright holder.

Susi Moore asserts her moral right to be identified as the author of this work

CHAPTER 1

'You're sure?' he asked.

My eyes were drawn to the glimmer at the centre of the lake. There, proud and luminous, stood the statue of Neptune. Beneath the imperious sea god, pulsed the lights of the secret, underwater ballroom.

'I want this meeting,' I said.

'You're not afraid?'

'Not one bit,' I lied.

It was past midnight on the eve of Valentine's. As agreed, Nathan led me to the entrance, which had long been camouflaged by storm severed branches and overgrown grasses. Buckled sections of highly ornate railings were strewn either side of us. A telltale reminder of times past?

I tried to imagine how this extraordinary Victorian ballroom had once been, with wealthy men and their beautiful mistresses. Had they lined up excitedly under the stars to gain passage to this most discreet venue d'amour? Perhaps their spirits danced here still.

The pathway began to slope down quite sharply, until we reached a rotunded construction. Its walls were covered in so much foliage it was hard to believe this strange, buried turret had ever been man-made. We carefully negotiated our way down moss strewn steps until we reached a curved, iron screen which shielded a solid oak door. I counted eighteen steps in all.

Nathan produced a set of keys and tackled the rusted padlock. As the lock scraped and clicked, he used his shoulders to force the door open. We stepped inside. Long undisturbed dust mites rose and fell as startled bats suddenly fluttered overhead.

I turned to my guide. I was ready to continue. Without words, he beckoned me to follow. As we walked down, muted light flickered from the base of the precipitous, winding stairwell, creating fleeting shadows across the walls. I counted a further eighteen steps.

We reached what appeared to be a circular holding chamber. There were several musty-smelling settees, cabinets and small tables. Subtle, artificial lighting flared on and off to the sound of intermittent buzzing. Nathan kept his spotlight switched on. 'Wiring needs attention,' he observed.

I walked around the holding room and paused at a section which had been hollowed through. There was a further set of steps forming a narrow gully downwards.

Nathan was at my side. 'Shall we?'

He took the lead as we went down to the lower level of the subterranean walkway. Another twelve steps.

We now faced the aperture of the most exquisitely lit, glistening white marble tunnel. The shaft, with its smoothly hewn walls and exotic, curved apex, had been built to extend from one end of the lake to the other. Gilded two seater canapés and large, sweeping parlour palms were at equal intervals as far as the eye could see.

I found myself thinking again about the illicit liaisons of those who came here so long ago, and whether their affairs had survived.

As we neared the centre, we could hear the muted throb of music. Nathan stopped in his tracks, turned to face me and shook my hand; 'I've taken you this far, Dr Westbrook. The rest is for you.'

'You're leaving?'

'I've escorted you, at great personal risk to myself. I need not remind you it will mean certain dismissal from my employers should they find out.'

He was right, of course. Nathan was the head caretaker for the Neptune Estate owners. He knew every nook and cranny of the great house and every inch of the landscape surrounding it. Should the existence of the ballroom be revealed to the general public, it would create unwelcome attention from hoards of press, tourists or worse.

'Goodnight, Dr Westbrook. I assure you, you will find what you want.'

He turned and walked away.

'Nathan?'

The sound of my voice ricocheted from floor to ceiling.

CHAPTER 2

Discordant snatches of music and conversation echoed through my head with such force that I thought I might lose consciousness. I raised my hands over my ears but there was no escape. I felt myself reel as my surroundings dissolved into a deafening, spiralling vortex.

'Freya?'

I was lying on a sofa. I looked up to see my sister.

'Laurie?' I gasped. *'Laurie?* Where are we?'

'The room,' she answered.

'What room?'

She looked as frail as ever. Her hair was long and pale ash blonde, her skin waxen, her eyes dull. She wore her favourite turquoise organza dress. The one we buried her in, only months before.

'I've been detained,' she smiled, a serene, desolate smile.

'Detained…?'

'In the space,' she said, 'between life and …'

'Laurie … I don't understand … this isn't real … you're not …'

'Freya,' she said, her voice weighted down. 'Please don't do what you're about to do.'

'No, don't say that. You can't say that. You never understood. Never. Don't even try to stop me …'

I began to feel light-headed, even queasy. I could no longer speak. My eyes stayed focussed on Laurie's face until all I became aware of was her large, sepulchral eyes.

Her expression was one of despondency. She was right. My intentions tonight were purely selfish. I was here to win back the man I loved, no matter what the cost.

Reverberations of music and laughter rose all around. The intensity was terrifying. I felt myself sink back down onto the sofa cushions.

Then, only blackness.

CHAPTER 3

I came to, with a jolt, at the very spot where Nathan had left me. Carefully, I rose to my feet and took a mirror from my bag to check my appearance. I dabbed a tissue at the smudged kohl beneath my eyes, spiked up my ash-blonde hair and smoothed down my black funnel-neck coat. If my mind had been playing tricks with me that was fine, but I had a meeting to attend. I set off down the tunnel, towards the centre of the lake.

It wasn't long before I reached the final aperture to step down a further six steps. The smell of damp and decay escalated.

I shivered, hands clutching my upper arms in an instinctive gesture. There, before me, in all its surreal splendour, was the entrance to the grand underwater ballroom. I took a deep breath and stepped forward.

I stood, open-mouthed beneath the great iron and glass dome.

Spotlights siphoned shimmering hues of turquoise from the expanse above onto the mirror-smooth floor below. Settees, upholstered in purple and gold were set around the periphery, alongside great trailing parlour palms. Sculptured nudes of gods and goddesses gazed coolly outwards from their marble pedestals.

I shuddered involuntarily. It was too cold, even for the dead.

There were roses, garnet red, meticulously arranged in beautiful amphoras. More were strewn over the sofas and side tables. Their heady perfume mingled with, rather than masked the torpid stench of rot.

At the far end of the ballroom, there was an ornate dais with music stands, a grand piano and crimson velvet seats.

Yet more roses. Someone was making an effort.

Then I heard it. Discordant ... wavering, straining sounds. Violins?

'Hello?' I called out.

Nothing, except a sudden muffled thud on the glass above. I looked up as vacuous, unblinking eyes peered down at me. More and more appeared. Sleek, dark, mesmerising shapes, warily drawn to the lights.

The sound of violins rose again, as though on a loop, winding and unwinding.

With a sudden, frenzied twisting and turning, the shoal of curious carp above fled.

I was alone. There was nothing here. I couldn't keep allowing my imagination to run away with me. My eyes were drawn to the marble archways at the far side of the dais. I decided to investigate.

Each archway was intricately carved and acted as a small but grand entrance to the ballroom antechambers.

The first contained a finely stocked bar with crystal decanters and exotic bottles of every shape, size and colour.

I heard a long sigh. I froze. Then there was the low hum of whispered chatter. A man coughing … a woman laughing. The hum rose and fell, then muted altogether. I don't know how long I stayed, rooted to the same spot, straining to hear anything at all. Only silence. Finally, I plucked up the courage to explore further.

The second chamber appeared to be a traditional gentleman's smoking lounge, furnished with impressive bookcases, dark red leather wingback chairs and mahogany side-tables.

Each of the chambers were sealed over in a beautifully ornate, scaled down version of the main glass dome.

I decided to sit and wait, and poured myself a generous glass of claret to boot. I allowed myself to gaze upwards at the spectacle of glinting, carp-free waters. I took a few sips of wine. Then a few more.

I sat back in my chair. Images of my lover filled my head. He was the reason I was here, after all.

I closed my eyes and thought back to when we first met.

CHAPTER 4

I'd been ambitious from an early age which meant I had little time for relationships. Oliver had been a patient at the practice, complaining of a flare-up of an old sports injury. I knew I was attracted to him, but I was a professional. Moreover, he was married. I put him out of my head. Then, one night, I ran into him at a fundraising event. As we spoke, he seemed to want to open up. He told me that his wife, Anna, following her first husband's suicide, had become withdrawn, to the point of catatonic. The only consolation was that she had been left well provided for, but she seemed hardly aware of it.

Oliver had been a business acquaintance of her husband and he decided to spend time with the new widow. He set about charming her back into a state of functionality and persuaded her it would benefit them both if she were to invest capital into his flagging overseas ventures. She duly invested and his fortunes were turned around. He didn't want to lose his now very best friend. He found himself proposing and they were married.

It wasn't too long though before she reverted to her clinical state, needing constant medication. She couldn't be left alone. Her parents had to stay when he was away on business. In time, he felt drained. He made a difficult decision. When the time was right, he would leave.

Then, one day, she looked him directly in the eyes, clasped her hand around his, drew it to her lips and kissed his fingertips. He was immediately taken aback.

'I know,' she said. 'I'm so sorry. Please don't go …'

All at once, he began to feel guilty.

He tried to make amends, do the right thing by her. He sought out treatment from the best experts and took her on extended breaks to the most exotic locations.

Surely, besides visits to the specialists, constant stimulation and kindness were all she needed?

But she couldn't ever fully shake off the mire of her disease. On her few lucid days he worried she was becoming suicidal.

He blamed himself. He felt helpless. He felt miserable.

He'd tried. But it wasn't enough. It never would be. More guilt. That's when my heart went out to him. I foolishly threw caution to the wind. I liked being in his company. He seemed to welcome mine.

CHAPTER 5

In the beginning, we saw each other wherever and whenever we could. He even rented out a little cottage in the country and we played at being a couple, in our own idyllic space, far removed from reality. In the actual world, I pursued my career while his home life remained unmarred. Over time, of course, I wanted more. Out came the classic ultimatum. Her or me. But he was too invested in his relationship with Anna, financially, and through guilt. So, he would stay with to her, no matter what. Goodbye cottage. Goodbye relationship. Goodbye Freya.

My world was turned upside down. I should have gone straight out and met someone else, but I was broken-hearted. I barely slept for months, and in the end, my day to day existence was just that.

I look back now and see how deluded I was.

Two months after our break-up, the caretaker from the nearby shambling Victorian country estate approached me at a garden fundraiser. He introduced himself as Nathan and seemed an odd, but harmless sort of fellow. He was having various minor health issues, which he decided to discuss with me a great length. I was quite bemused but it was not uncommon in my job, on duty or not. I offered informal advice. I didn't stop to think how he knew me but his gratitude knew no bounds.

'I have an acquaintance,' he said, 'who can make the impossible become possible. Think carefully. If you need his services, come to me.'

It seemed a little strange, but I thanked him. If anyone needed the impossible to become possible at this point, it was me. I knew now that my ex-lover's sense of practicalities prevented him from ever leaving his despondent wife. It was easier to allow the drugs to desensitise her while he spent much time away on business. He would continue to play the good husband out of his tangled sense of duty and guilt.

I smiled ruefully. The only thing that could help me right now would be to make a deal with the devil himself.

I had many vivid dreams that night, until at one point, I woke up dripping in a cold, sweat. My limbs felt like lead. I thought I heard whispers, voices, calling my name. My stomach suddenly lurched. I felt a terrifying sense of vertigo as though my soul was rising from my body. I wanted to cry out but it was impossible.

No, no, my thoughts screamed. *Not now. I'm not ready.*

'Oh, but you are,' a voice rasped.

I couldn't answer. I couldn't make any sound at all.

'Listen carefully,' the voice continued. 'These are my terms.'

CHAPTER 6

I tossed and turned for the rest of the night. Still shaken, I rose early. The phone rang. It was Nathan from the garden fundraiser. I hadn't remembered giving him my number.

'I trust you slept well, Doctor Westbrook?'

'What? Why do you ask?'

'Doctor Westbrook,' the caretaker spoke quietly. 'I only want to help. My acquaintance, he has the means. Do you really want to carry on as you are?'

'Why would you ask me that?'

'I don't think you do,' he went on. 'Think things over. Your case will be treated with the utmost discretion.'

CHAPTER 7

So here I was, in this underworld which held the souls of all the adulterers who had made their deals before me.

'A spectacular folly, this ballroom, don't you think?'

I started in shock, my heart beating wildly. I'd come here to meet someone no one would wish to meet. I'd heard no sound, no footsteps, but the Devil was now in front of me. I was taken aback by his appearance. He was tall, fine boned, with glacier white skin and sleek, glossed black hair. He wore a high collared white dress shirt beneath an expensively woven midnight blue suit. The only affectation of sartorial indifference was a carelessly folded damson silk cravat.

'This fantasia under the lake was created over a hundred years ago by one of England's most eccentric businessman.'

His voice was mesmerising, with its own unearthly resonance.

'He became, shall we say, *over* eccentric and was eventually convicted of obscene amounts of fraud.'

The eyes of the Devil glittered with preternatural brilliance, and never left mine.

'After sentencing, he took a cyanide pill. So obliging ...'

'I heard the stories ...' I said, finally finding my voice.

My host grinned disarmingly.

'He now resides here. Had you heard *that*? A guest in his own home.'

I regarded him as though indulging an inventive child.

'I actually quite enjoy his company ...' he added, pausing for a reaction.

I said nothing.

He changed tack. 'You don't mind if I smoke?'

I indicated he do so. His eyes flashed, a clear cerulean-turquoise.

'Rolled in Honduras in 1908. One of my other protégés...' he smiled, broadly, revealing perfect white teeth.

With long-practised finesse, he placed a large cigar between his finely formed lips. Tendrils of thick, curling smoke rose around us. I found the smooth, peaty aroma strangely calming and used the few seconds to steady myself.

'You're ... *young* ... ' I began.

'You're surprised? It is ... of course, a perk of my vocation.' He smiled his most engaging smile yet.

'I see ... And what do I call you?'

'So many names! So many nuances. Yet, I digress. I always liked *Ramiel* ... yes ... *Ramiel, the escorter of souls.* It has a certain flourish, don't you think?'

'Ramiel ... ' I repeated, allowing the syllables to roam around my mouth.

'You came here to offer me something?'

'Yes,' I answered, 'I have.'

'On this eve of Saint Valentine's?' He smiled. 'So delicious! So *inappropriate* ...'

He paused to select a rose and carefully glided his fingertips up the thorn-ridden stem. He seemed momentarily pre-occupied as, head tilted, he took in the heavy scent of the flower. Then his gaze returned to mine.

Fingers bloodied, he passed the bloom to me.

We looked at each for a few drawn-out beats. I put the rose down. He pulled a laced handkerchief from his top pocket and dabbed at his cuts. I could smell his blood, pungent and warm.

'Well, where do we start? Your illicit lover? He cared for you?'

I had to blink and look away. Was it heartbreak … or guilt? Maybe it was both. Maybe it was neither. But I was certain of one thing, my lover had feelings for me.

'Yes, he did.'

'You believed him?'

'He said he couldn't live without me.'

'You BELIEVED him?'

'I didn't just jump into …'

Well, maybe I did. No, I didn't.

'Then why?' the Devil asked.

'We were lonely. We were drawn to each other.'

'Oh, so touching.' my host mocked. 'So sad. Have you met her? The only unfortunate in this ménage à trois?'

'Never. She rarely goes out. She has … demons.'

'Really? We must be introduced! So, you think he pities her?'

'She came from a wealthy family. He was sinking in debt. She helped him. He married her.'

'You know a lot about a woman who doesn't venture out?'

'I know what he's told me. Why would he lie? I just try to put it all together, to make sense of it.'

'You feel he sacrifices his happiness to repay a debt?'

'He wouldn't see it that way.'

'Ahh, the upkeep of the façade! And you, sweet Freya, so earnest, so *sérieux,* How do you fit in?'

'I was caught up in my career. I made no time for … There was just something about him …'

'You made no effort to walk away?'

'At first, but the attraction was too strong.'

'Stop it! Priceless!'

'Loneliness distorts everything. I wouldn't expect you to understand.'

'What? Your excuses are abominable. You think I don't understand loneliness in my line of work? You don't know the half of it.'

'Really? *You* don't know the half of it …'

My host suddenly became serious. 'When you fall in love, choice is never clear cut or rational. It seems to me you sacrificed all quality of life for this exemplary trickster.'

'Am I hearing sympathy ... *from* the devil?'

'*Please ...*'

'I don't care,' I said. 'He's not what you think, and I came here to make a deal.'

'At last! We get to the crux of things! More wine?'

He poured us both a generous measure. As the claret coursed down my throat, I knew I was right to want more from life.

'I thought I was ... helping him,' I said.

My host cocked his head, eyes shining in bemusement.

'Wondrous! So now you think you're the noble one?'

'I thought ... in time ...'

'In time, in time? Infidelity is neither the act of love or duty.'

Sudden, surprising tears began to well up.

'You ... the Devil, lecturing *me*?' I managed to shoot back, wiping my eyes.

My host leaned forwards. His fingertips brushed my cheekbone with a softness I hadn't expected.

'*He* is without principle. I, on the other hand would crawl over broken glass to have a female like you at my side. Are you sure this mortal man is worth it?'

I could almost taste the blood from the rose thorns.

'Yes,' I said, regaining my composure. 'Yes.'

My host sighed an exasperated sigh. 'Then, to business. Have you thought about my offer?'

'I have ...'

'You want to be *her*?'

'With my whole being.'

'You believe I have the *power*?'

'I believe.'

My host regarded me a little longer. 'I think the love you feel is real. Yet, he is cowardly and you are bled dry. I would normally take your soul without remorse, but today, I give you this last chance.'

I took a deep mouthful of wine.

'Let me illustrate, again, how this works. You will swap places. Your soul, your essence, your spirit will leave your physical body and will enter hers. Ergo, her soul, essence and spirit will leave her body and enter yours. The bonus? She will lose all memory of her former life, but you will have yours!

Your Oliver will come home, dutifully to his wife, who is now you. Your personality will obliterate all that has gone before and he'll marvel at the change. He'll fall head over heels in love, with you, in her body, and only *you* will know why! No more living in the shadows, no more half-life. The only change will be in your physical appearance. He'll be happy because love will overtake duty. You'll be happy because love will overtake duty. What could go wrong?'

I couldn't wait.

'You understand the price?' he asked.

'I understand. My soul. When I die, you take my soul.'

His lips curved into that smile. 'It's been my pleasure to offer such a ... creative solution to your problem. But, Freya Westbrook, at this point, you still have a choice. Think carefully.'

I sighed. 'Can I ask why we had to meet here, at this ungodly hour?'

'Ungodly being the operative word? To test you. To see how much you really wanted this. You passed.'

I could feel his gaze take my measure from head to toe.

I took another sip of the warming claret. 'I heard violins ...' I said, finally, to break the silence.

He arched his brow and studied me intently. I didn't flinch as he took my hand in his. 'Come,' he said. 'Let's take a moment.' His eyes became luminous in the reflection of the florescent waters all around us. A tendril of hair dropped over his forehead.

I allowed him to lead me back into the ballroom. A quintet of shabbily suited musicians were already seated on the music dais. Unearthly inflections of violin strings arose.

We turned to face each other as the long, searing notes, both mournful and tender, echoed throughout the dome. The Devil placed his arm around my waist and drew me to him. I could feel his heart pounding through his chest. We moved in unison. His body in close proximity exuded a litheness I'd never experienced before. His eyes never left mine. I felt strangely calm and strangely intoxicated.

His lips suddenly brushed the nape of my neck, up to my face and then onto my open mouth. His lips were soft, his mouth explored mine and my senses reeled. I made myself take a step back but he took my hand and pressed his fingers through mine. I knew he wanted me and in that moment, I think I wanted him.

'Ramiel,' I said. 'Our deal … just our deal.'

There was only the sound of our breathing.

His expression became cold. After what seemed an age, he dropped my hand and stood aside.

'A pity. Goodnight, Freya Westbrook. I look forward with interest to our next … rendezvous.'

'That won't be for a very long time,' I said.

He looked at me hard, searching every inch of my face.

'I wouldn't bank on it,' he replied.

CHAPTER 8

The sound of my spike heels echo-bulleted through the tunnel as I rushed back towards the iron stairwell. I got to the top of the turret and pounded at the door until it opened. Once outside, I ran up the winding stone stops, onto the pathway and past the old iron railings. Breathing hard, I took one last look at the lake, barely perceiving the outline of the statue of Neptune on its watery dais. Everything was shrouded in darkness.

I drove back home. There was little point in going to bed. My shift at the clinic would start in a few hours. I showered, had breakfast and went to work.

By nightfall, my lack of sleep was catching up with me. I made a light supper and went to bed.

'Anna?'

'Ollie?' I looked around. It was early morning, I was in a bed, but it wasn't my bed. I took a deep breath. 'Ollie ... It's *me* ...'

'Well, of course it's you. Who else would it be? I like you calling me Ollie! That's different. Come down to breakfast. I have a surprise for you.'

I rose out of bed. I felt so odd in this new body. I looked into the wardrobe mirrors and saw her. A young woman with long, luxuriant copper tresses, slim, petite and beautiful.

He hadn't told me how beautiful she was.

I thought of my own tousled wisps of ash blonde hair. Would I come to miss it in time? I picked up the silk dressing gown from the bottom of the bed and made my way downstairs. Breakfast was laid out. He indicated I sit down at the table. My heart sank as I saw there was a card and a single red rose stem in front of me, with more rose stems scattered about the room.

'We're on our own,' he announced, conspiratorially. 'I've given the help the day off.'

'Oh ...' It was the sound of *her* voice coming from her lips. Not mine.

'It's just you and me.'

'Aren't you working?' I ventured.

'On Valentine's? When do I ever work on Valentine's? But then, we hardly need an excuse. Our staff adore us, we give them so many days off. With pay, I might add.' He beamed the handsome grin I knew so well. He stood behind my chair and impulsively bent down to kiss the top of my head.

'Ollie, I'm a little confused ...'

'No confusion here,' he said.

'Wait ...'

'Lost your appetite? Good. How about I carry you back up those stairs?'

'Ollie? No ...'

'Yes,' he countered, becoming serious. 'Oh, yes…'

My lover leaned over me, and spread my dressing gown back, exposing the nape of my neck. Her neck. He pressed his lips against my skin, so tenderly, and then with more urgency, down to my shoulders, allowing his hands to stray onto my breasts. Her breasts.

He had lied to me all this time. He was besotted with his wife. I had caught him in the act. I was the act.

I pulled her dressing gown around my shoulders and straightened up. 'I'm Freya, Ollie. *Not* Anna.'

'What?'

'*Freya,*' I repeated.

Ollie fixed his gaze on me and spoke slowly and deliberately. 'I honestly don't know what you mean.'

'I AM FREYA. That's what I mean. I am the woman you loved. I am the woman you said you couldn't be without, and now, I'm forced to witness THIS? How could you have lied to me all this time?' My voice, her voice, was breaking up in near sobs.

'Anna, I think you're getting terribly mixed up. We can fix this. I don't know who told you about any Freya but they've got completely the wrong end of the stick. Good God, Anna, where would I find time to be with anyone else. You wear me out, I wear you out. We can't keep our hands off each other. How could I ever want to be with anyone else?'

The pain of his words was unbearable.

'How could I want to be with you after this?' I shot back. I ran upstairs and began sifting through the wardrobes, looking for something to wear. He followed me.

'Leave me alone,' I sobbed.

'No, Anna, never. You can't let stupid gossip upset you like this! That's all it is. I hardly know who they would mean. Who on earth is Freya, anyway?'

'Who? She's your doctor!' I screamed back at him. 'I'M your doctor! I'm Freya.'

'You're driving me crazy. What's wrong with you? Anna, come here.' He scooped me into his arms and placed me onto the bed and placed himself over me. 'There, that's better. Now we're going to talk properly. I don't want to have to pin you down like this but I need you to hear me out. I've only ever known Doctor Westbrook as Doctor Westbrook. Her first name is Freya? News to me. Now let's just be sensible.'

I tried to struggle away from him but he was too strong.

'Let's have no more of this. Look at me, no, look at me. We've had a perfect five years together. Perfect. I could not be a more lucky man. Why would I ever do anything that I know would hurt you and risk losing ... everything?'

He was good. I nearly believed him. I would have believed him, but I was Freya, not Anna, and I now knew how well he could lie.

'Anna, I think we're ready now to have children, lots and lots of them. Let me prove to you how much I love you.'

He began nuzzling his mouth into my neck and onto my shoulders. The comfort and familiarity of his natural body scent was momentarily intoxicating. His hands found their way inside my dressing gown and his fingertips explored my bare skin.

'Anna, I want us to have a baby…'

'Stop,' I said, 'Stop!'

He released me with a truly convincing look of hurt and bewilderment on his face.

I flew to the wardrobe, grabbed the first outfit I could see and locked myself in the adjacent bathroom.

'What are you doing?' he demanded.

'I'm leaving. I'm going home.'

'You ARE home.'

'No, I'm not, I'm not home at all.'

Dressed, I hurtled past him to snatch the handbag that was on the dressing table and ran down the stairs. He ran down after me and pleaded with me to come back, but I didn't respond. I was through the front door and out. There was a main road not too far ahead.

I found a little money inside the handbag and hailed a taxi.

I was going back to the Neptune Estate, back to see the Devil's lackey.

CHAPTER 9

I hammered on the front door of the main house. A butler answered and regarded me a little apprehensively.

'I need to speak to Nathan.'

'Nathan, madam? There is no Nathan here.'

'Of course there is. Let him know I'm here.'

'And, you are?'

'Doctor Westbrook, Doctor Freya Westbrook, ask him, he knows who I am.'

'Please wait,' the butler said, closing the door.

After a few minutes, the butler returned. 'I'm afraid I'll have to ask you to leave, madam, we don't want any trouble.'

'Doctor ... not madam, *Doctor* Westbrook ...'

'Yes, of course you are. Can I ask why you want to see the caretaker, madam?'

'It's a private matter. Extremely urgent.'

'The thing is, madam, we've never had a Nathan. We did have a *Nathaniel* ... but he disappeared many years ago. Strange, dreadful business ... Do you think you've been getting confused?'

I was getting asked that question a lot today.

'Who is your current caretaker?'

'He's over in the walled garden behind the old kitchens, madam. I think there's been some trouble with trespassers.'

'Can you please point me in the right direction? I'll go and speak to him myself.'

The butler grudgingly obliged, telling me he'd radio the caretaker to let him know I was on the way.

I found the kitchen garden. I introduced myself to Peter, the 'present' caretaker, who looked at me a little oddly. It dawned on me that introducing myself as Doctor Westbrook was not strictly correct, but it was too late now.

'I wonder if you can help me, Peter. I was looking for Nathan. He's been the caretaker here for a while. He's been helping me ...'

Peter looked as baffled as the butler. 'I'm sorry, but there's no Nathan here now. I've been caretaker here for over twenty years, and before that there was Harry.'

'You're quite sure? There's never been an employee, or anyone here called Nathan?'

'Absolutely sure, not in my time, anyway. The butler told me what he'd told you, that there'd been a Nathaniel here a good while ago, but that's it.'

I sighed. 'He also says you've been having problems with trespassers?'

'Ah, yes, well, yes, indeed, madam, but nothing we can't handle.'

'I've heard rumours, Peter, about some kind of underwater ballroom? Have you ever heard anything?'

He hesitated. 'Well, that's just the problem, madam. These trespassers have also heard rumours and they're starting to come from far and wide.'

'You must know about it? Haven't you ever seen it?'

'It's not for me to say.'

'Help me, please. I promise it won't go any further.' I began to cry, softly, in frustration. Did Anna always cry so softly?

Peter took a long look at me. I must have looked extremely appealing, with my full, ruby lips quivering and wisps of my long red hair blowing about my face. Or, Anna's face.

'Don't get so upset, dear. You seem to be in earnest. I'll tell you what I know. You are right. There are stories that, every so often, if you stand on the embankments late at night, you can see the glow of swirling lights, right from the centre of the lake. Right from under the statue of Neptune itself. Rather fanciful stories, don't you think? I, for one, though, have never seen anything like that,' he added with a wink.

It was no use. I needed Nathan.

I thanked Peter and headed off to the lakeside myself to search for the entrance I'd used, from only a few nights before.

I found the fallen railings. Without a backwards glance, I took the pathway down to the turret entrance. The padlock remained unfastened. None of this was making sense. I pushed through the old door. There was little time. I sped down the steep, spiral staircase.

CHAPTER 10

'Freya? Freya?'

My sister gazed down at me.

'Laurie?'

'We're in the waiting room, Freya.'

It all seemed oddly familiar. The room ... the room between heaven and ...

Oh no.

'There's nothing more I can do,' she said.

'Laurie ... I'

'I have to go.' There was a disturbing finality in her tone.

'Go? You can't leave me now ...'

'It's my time, and yours.'

I could feel tears welling up. 'Laurie? Laurie?'

'I'm so sorry, Freya.'

There was the vacuum of strange music and deafening reverberations. Was it happening again? Everything whirled around me. The waiting room was gone. Laurie was gone. There was absolutely nothing.

I was at the bottom of the stairwell. I felt a strange mixture of numbness and nausea. I heard voices overhead. I was cold. I heard my own voice scream out.

All went to black.

CHAPTER 11

I found my way back to the dome.

'Well, well, what have we here?' Ramiel, the seasoned showman, inclined his head of newly tousled hair. His jacket was swung over the back of a settee. He took out cigar and placed it securely between his lips.

My sense of nausea still with me, I hovered in front of him, gasping.

'It was worse than I could ever have imagined,' I said. 'He lied about everything. They had a full relationship, very full, in fact.'

'Hah! How utterly regrettable! So, how does this affect … *our* relationship?'

'I can't stay with him, knowing how he loves her. You have to reverse everything.'

He seemed surprised. 'And you, Freya, know the terms.'

'He *tricked* me …'

The Devil almost howled. 'How odd, that *he* should be the swindler, and I, the one to keep my word!' He drew at his cigar and smiled broadly, as though this was all a charming contretemps.

Something made me look upwards. Shoals of sinewy carp stared down, with stupefied, unblinking eyes. Ramiel followed my gaze then cocked his head sideways. I couldn't stand any more.

'You must change us back ...'

'I must? I MUST? You fell in love with this fool. You could have stayed with me and had everything. But, no, with your precious, misplaced feelings, you had to run off and play out your ridiculous charade. I should quite admire someone who thrives on such deception. We have *so* much in common ...'

'The deal is off,' I retorted.

'Off? Off? I thought you were an intelligent woman? Did you not just see your dear departed sister?'

'Laurie?'

'Sweet Laurie! Did you not see her, after you slipped from the steps of this underwater hell mouth… ' He drew at his cigar and tendrils of smoke swirled over us.

'Slipped?'

'And snapped your neck …' he smiled convivially.

'You're bluffing. Deception is your art.'

'Hah! So amusing. But, you *are* dead. Quite dead.'

'Our deal *is* off …'

'I love this part,' he said, eyes gleaming. 'When the dead cannot see that they are … dead. Let me explain. Only your spirit, an image, a *representation* of you, is here in front of me.'

The seconds ticked away as we stared at each other.

'Why ... your feet aren't even touching the floor.' He enunciated each word with rising malevolence.

The numbness. The nausea. The chills ...

'Don't you *feel* different?' he enquired.

I sobbed out loud. He was serious. Deadly serious. I turned and flew around the dome, screaming in despair.

'And now you're flying. Literally. I've given you something only a few can ever have after death. You have *form,* dear Freya, with benefits,' he said, eyes glittering.

I was in front of him. Shivering. Otherworldly face to otherworldly face.

'You're experiencing shock right now. Quite understandable. But you will adjust, Freya. You won't feel the nausea forever. At least, not all of the time, anyway.'

'My ... soul? What about my soul?'

'Really? Must you ask? Your mortal soul is mine. Let me tell you about me. I bargain with every soul I can lay my hands on. Some are murderers, some are thieves, and some, like you, are fools. Millennia in, millennia out, I get ever more disenchanted. I like to be entertained, Freya, especially where lovers are concerned! So, every

Valentine's Day, the lights go up, the orchestra plays and the spirits of my guests take their old form and dance ...'

'So the rumours ... the stories ...' I said. 'WHY? Why would you ... why would *they?*'

'*They* are caught in a collective of dreams and memories, a continuum of their own choosing. Rather than rise to heaven or sink to hell, they relive the same night, over and over. They are the Lorelei that draw in your curious, burning young hearts and more importantly, your souls, to be traded for shimmering immortality. I quite literally get a charge from it!'

'You can't get away with ...'

'Oh, but I think I can. You made a special journey all the way down here to make this very deal. A pity. You could have been my consort. As one, we could have made much *phantasmagoric* music ...'

My head was reeling. 'I won't live like *this.*'

'Unfortunate choice of words. Would you like to hear it in the current parlance? *FYI*, I was *always* going to take your soul. You didn't think the other fellow, my opposite number, would get it, did you?'

'You're lying ...'

'Really? Really? Speaking of liars, maybe we should get that lover of yours down here, he's a piece of work, eh? I'll resurrect Nathaniel and put him to task. What do you say? Who knows, for next Valentine's, you and sweet Ollie could be reunited.'

I swallowed hard, wretched and helpless as the Devil continued.

'Oh, but you won't look like *you*, will you? You'll look like *her!* Too bad. I can picture it now. Roses. So *many* roses! A crimson silk dress for you and a sombre black suit for him. Well, he *will* be deceased! You can dance together, here, in this splendid hell mouth, under the lake, for all eternity.'

I opened my mouth to speak but the only sound that came was a long, piercing wail.

'Come now, it's not *that* bad! Let's celebrate, you and I. Drink?'

THE END

POSTSCRIPT

A real-life underwater ballroom lies 40 feet beneath a lake between Godalming and Haslemere in Surrey. James Whitaker Wright, silver mining entrepreneur, created the underwater pleasure dome in the late 1890s. Following exposure for a financial scam that ruined many of his investors, he smoked a cigar after his trial at the Royal Courts of Justice and promptly committed suicide by cyanide poisoning.

These days, the underwater ballroom lies empty, with only the carp for company, while the statue of Neptune guards over what was once a most lavish symbol of Victorian opulence.

* * * * * * *

IMAGE / visualnews.com

IMAGE / visualnews.com

REVIEW EXTRACTS

http://amzn.to/2b7NbAu

(AMAZON UK)

'MYSTERIOUS, ENIGMATIC ... FUSED WITH DARK EXPECTANCY ...'

'A NEPTUNIAN, DREAM-LIKE, PAST WORLD OF HIGH GLAMOUR AND ROMANCE ...'

'EVOCATIVE, WITTY, BRUTAL ...'

'IF YOU LIKE STORIES WITH A TWIST, THEN THIS AUTHOR HAS THEM.'

IMAGE / visualnews.com

A special thank you to my daughters,

Emma, Kate & Lucy

♥

Precious and treasured.

The Secret Ballroom © 2015 Susi Moore.
All Rights Reserved.
ISBN 978-154416773

No part of this work or publication may be reproduced in any form
without the prior written permission
of the copyright holder.

Susi Moore asserts her moral right to be
identified as the author of this work.

MUSE, IMAGINE,
CREATE & WRITE ...
© 2016 Susi Moore

The Secret Ballroom is taken from an upcoming collection of short stories exploring rituals, whether a euphoric gathering on the summer solstice or strange events on a winter's night.

ALSO AVAILABLE BY SUSI MOORE

LEVANA'S WISH
http://amzn.to/2buF9CL

FLEUR (A PARISIENNE HAUNTING)
https://t.co/DUxWIuZ0Wz

COMING UP

LEVANA'S DREAM

For author updates: https://twitter.com/MuserScribe

Susi Moore on Amazon: http://amzn.to/2b7NbAu

Susi Moore's upcoming collection of stories is for lovers of supernatural, romantic and literary fiction.

Titles include 'Levana's Wish', 'The Secret Ballroom' and the double-category award-nominated 'Fleur - A Parisienne Haunting'.

Ms Moore has been writing since she can remember. She received early acclaim when her music teacher once asked her to stand on a chair and improvise a story to occupy a (quite) fractious end of year class! More recently, as well as her day job and raising a family, she's produced writing workshops for her local college, designed an online course for E-Novelist, runs 'MuserScribe', (musings for aspiring writers) and tends to the whims of her artful felines, Marley and Tabitha.

She's currently working on several projects, including completion of her anthology.

Susi Moore - Amazon UK:
http://amzn.to/2b7NbAu

Susi Moore - Amazon USA:
https://www.amazon.com/author/musermoore

Website:
https://susiwritingmooreuk.wordpress.com

For author updates, musings, original writing prompts and more:
https://twitter.com/MuserScribe

© 2016 Susi Moore

© MUSERSCRIBE PUBLISHING

* * * * * * *